# THE
# TALES
## OF
# BEEDLE
## THE
# BARD

*Translated from the Ancient Runes by*
# HERMIONE GRANGER

*Commentary by*
# ALBUS DUMBLEDORE

*Introduction, Notes, and Illustrations by*
# J. K. ROWLING

children's
## HIGH LEVEL GROUP

*In association with*
## ARTHUR A. LEVINE BOOKS
An Imprint of Scholastic Inc.

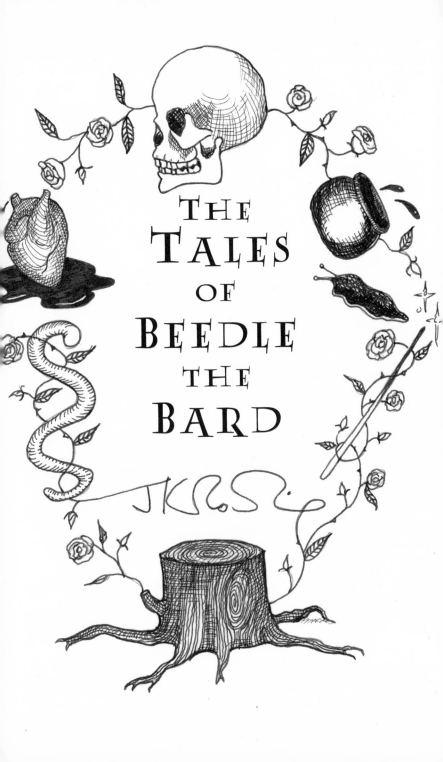

# The Tales of Beedle the Bard

Library of Congress Control Number: 2008934360

ISBN-13: 978-0-545-12828-5 · ISBN-10: 0-545-12828-5

10 9 8 7 6 5 4 3 2 1     08 09 10 11 12

Printed in the U.S.A. 55
First edition, December 2008

# CONTENTS

# INTRODUCTION

THE TALES OF BEEDLE THE BARD
is a collection of stories written for young
wizards and witches. They have been popular
bedtime reading for centuries, with the result
that the Hopping Pot and the Fountain of Fair
Fortune are as familiar to many of the students
at Hogwarts as Cinderella and Sleeping Beauty
are to Muggle (non-magical) children.

Beedle's stories resemble our fairy tales in
many respects; for instance, virtue is usually
rewarded, and wickedness punished. However,
there is one very obvious difference. In Muggle

fairy tales, magic tends to lie at the root of the hero's or heroine's troubles — the wicked witch has poisoned the apple, or put the princess into a hundred-year's sleep, or turned the prince into a hideous beast. In *The Tales of Beedle the Bard*, on the other hand, we meet heroes and heroines who can perform magic themselves, and yet find it just as hard to solve their problems as we do. Beedle's stories have helped generations of Wizarding parents to explain this painful fact of life to their young children: that magic causes as much trouble as it cures.

Another notable difference between these fables and their Muggle counterparts is that Beedle's witches are much more active in seeking their fortunes than our fairy-tale heroines. Asha, Altheda, Amata, and Babbitty Rabbitty are all witches who take their fates into their own hands, rather than taking a prolonged nap or waiting for someone to return a lost shoe. The exception to this rule — the unnamed maiden of "The Warlock's Hairy Heart" — acts more like our idea of a storybook princess, but there is no "happily ever after" at the end of her tale.

Beedle the Bard lived in the fifteenth century, and much of his life remains shrouded in mystery. We know that he was born in Yorkshire, and the only surviving woodcut shows that he had an exceptionally luxuriant beard. If his stories accurately reflect his opinions, he rather liked

Muggles, whom he regarded as ignorant rather than malevolent; he mistrusted Dark Magic, and he believed that the worst excesses of wizardkind sprang from the all-too-human traits of cruelty, apathy, or arrogant misapplication of their own talents. The heroes and heroines who triumph in his stories are not those with the most powerful magic, but rather those who demonstrate the most kindness, common sense, and ingenuity.

One modern-day wizard who held very similar views was, of course, Professor Albus Percival Wulfric Brian Dumbledore, Order of Merlin (First Class), Headmaster of Hogwarts School of Witchcraft and Wizardry, Supreme Mugwump of the International Confederation of Wizards, and Chief Warlock of the Wizengamot. This similarity of outlook notwithstanding, it was a surprise to discover a set of notes on *The Tales of Beedle the Bard* among the many papers that Dumbledore left in his will to the Hogwarts Archives. Whether this commentary was written for his own satisfaction or for future publication, we shall never know; however, we have been graciously granted permission by Professor Minerva McGonagall, now Headmistress of Hogwarts, to print Professor Dumbledore's notes here, alongside a brand-new translation of the *Tales* by Hermione Granger. We hope that Professor Dumbledore's insights, which include observations on Wizarding history, personal reminiscences, and enlightening information on key elements of each story, will help a new generation of both Wizarding and Muggle readers appreciate *The Tales of Beedle the Bard.* It is the belief of all who knew him personally that Professor Dumbledore would have been delighted to lend his support to this project, given that all royalties are to be donated to the Children's High Level Group, which works to benefit children in desperate need of a voice.

It seems only right to make one small, additional comment on Professor Dumbledore's notes. As far as we can tell, the notes were completed around eighteen months before the tragic events that took place at the top of Hogwarts's

Astronomy Tower. Those familiar with the history of the most recent Wizarding war (everyone who has read all seven volumes on the life of Harry Potter, for instance) will be aware that Professor Dumbledore reveals a little less than he knows — or suspects — about the final story in this book. The reason for any omission lies, perhaps, in what Dumbledore said about truth, many years ago, to his favorite and most famous pupil:

"It is a beautiful and terrible thing, and should therefore be treated with great caution."

Whether we agree with him or not, we can perhaps excuse Professor Dumbledore for wishing to protect future readers from the temptations to which he himself had fallen prey,

and for which he paid so terrible a price.

J. K. Rowling
2008

**A Note on the Footnotes**
Professor Dumbledore appears to have been writing
for a Wizarding audience, so I have occasionally
inserted an explanation of a term or fact that
might need clarification for Muggle readers.
— JKR —

# THE
# TALES
## OF
# BEEDLE
## THE
# BARD

# THE WIZARD AND
# THE HOPPING POT

There was once a kindly old wizard who used his magic generously and wisely for the benefit of his neighbors. Rather than reveal the true source of his power, he pretended that his potions, charms, and antidotes sprang ready-made from the little cauldron he called his lucky cooking pot. From miles around, people came to him with their troubles, and the wizard was pleased to give his pot a stir, and put things right.

This well-beloved wizard lived to a goodly age, then died, leaving all his chattels to his only son. This son was of a very different disposition to his gentle father. Those who could not work magic were, to the son's mind, worthless, and he had often quarreled with his father's habit of dispensing magical aid to their neighbors.

Upon the father's death, the son found hidden inside the old cooking pot a small package bearing his name. He opened it, hoping for gold, but found instead a soft, thick slipper, much too small to wear, and with no pair. A fragment of parchment within the slipper bore the words "In the fond hope, my son, that you will never need it."

The son cursed his father's age-softened mind, then threw the slipper back into the cauldron, resolving to use it henceforth as a rubbish pail.

That very night a peasant woman knocked on the front door.

"My granddaughter is afflicted by a crop of warts, sir," she told him. "Your father used to mix a special poultice in that old cooking pot —"

"Begone!" cried the son. "What care I for your brat's warts?"

And he slammed the door in the old woman's face.

At once there came a loud clanging and banging from his kitchen. The wizard lit his wand and opened the door, and there, to his amazement, he saw his father's old cooking pot: It had sprouted a single foot of brass, and was hopping on the spot in the middle of the floor, making a fearful noise upon the flagstones. The wizard approached it in wonder, but fell back hurriedly when he saw that the whole of the pot's surface was covered in warts.

"Disgusting object!" he cried, and he tried firstly to Vanish the pot, then to clean it by magic, and finally to force it out of the house. None of his spells worked, however, and he was unable to prevent the pot hopping after him out of the kitchen, and then following him up to bed, clanging and banging loudly on every wooden stair.

The wizard could not sleep all night for the banging of the warty old pot by his bedside, and next morning the pot insisted upon hopping after him to the breakfast table. *Clang, clang, clang* went the brass-footed pot, and the wizard had not even started his porridge when there came another knock on the door.

An old man stood on the doorstep.

"'Tis my old donkey, sir," he explained. "Lost, she is, or stolen, and without her I cannot take my wares to market, and my family will go hungry tonight."

"And I am hungry now!" roared the wizard, and he slammed the door upon the old man.

*Clang, clang, clang* went the cooking pot's single brass foot upon the floor, but now its clamor was mixed with the brays of a donkey and human groans of hunger, echoing from the depths of the pot.

"Be still. Be silent!" shrieked the wizard, but not all his magical powers could quieten the warty pot, which hopped at his heels all day, braying and groaning and clanging, no matter where he went or what he did.

That evening there came a third knock upon the door, and there on the threshold stood a young woman sobbing as though her heart would break.

"My baby is grievously ill," she said. "Won't you please help us? Your father bade me come if troubled —"

But the wizard slammed the door on her.

And now the tormenting pot filled to the brim with salt water, and slopped tears all over the floor as it hopped, and brayed, and groaned, and sprouted more warts.

Though no more villagers came to seek help at the wizard's cottage for the rest of the week, the pot kept him informed of their many ills. Within a few days it was not only braying and groaning and slopping and hopping and sprouting warts, it was also choking and retching, crying like a baby, whining like a dog, and spewing out bad cheese and sour milk and a plague of hungry slugs.

The wizard could not sleep or eat with the pot beside him, but the pot refused to leave, and he could not silence it or force it to be still.

At last the wizard could bear it no more.

"Bring me all your problems, all your troubles, and your woes!" he screamed, fleeing into the night, with the pot hopping behind him along the road into the village. "Come! Let me cure you, mend you, and comfort you! I have my father's cooking pot, and I shall make you well!"

And with the foul pot still bounding along behind him, he ran up the street, casting spells in every direction.

Inside one house the little girl's warts vanished as she slept; the lost donkey was Summoned from a distant briar patch and set down softly in its stable; the sick baby was doused in dittany and woke, well and rosy. At every house of sickness and sorrow the wizard did his best, and gradually the cooking pot beside him stopped groaning and retching, and became quiet, shiny, and clean.

"Well, Pot?" asked the trembling wizard as the sun began to rise.

The pot burped out the single slipper he had thrown into it, and permitted him to fit it onto the brass foot. Together, they set off back to the wizard's house, the pot's footstep muffled at last. But from that day forward, the wizard helped the villagers, like his father before him, lest the pot cast off its slipper, and begin to hop once more.

# ALBUS DUMBLEDORE

*on "The Wizard and the Hopping Pot"*

A kind old wizard decides to teach his hard-hearted son a lesson, by giving him a taste of the local Muggles' misery. The young wizard's conscience awakes, and he agrees to use his magic for the benefit of his non-magical neighbors. A simple and heartwarming fable, one might think — in which case, one would reveal oneself to be an innocent nincompoop. A pro-Muggle story showing a Muggle-loving father as superior in magic to a Muggle-hating son? It is nothing short of amazing that any copies of the original version of this tale surived the flames to which they were so often consigned.

Beedle was somewhat out of step with his times in preaching a message of brotherly love for Muggles. The persecution of witches and wizards was gathering pace all over Europe in the early fifteenth century. Many in the magical community felt, and with good reason, that offering to cast a spell on the Muggle next door's sickly pig was tantamount to volunteering to fetch the firewood for one's own funeral pyre.[1]

---

1 It is true, of course, that genuine witches and wizards were reasonably adept at escaping the stake, block, and noose (see my comments about Lisette de Lapin in the commentary on "Babbitty Rabbitty and Her Cackling Stump"). However, a number of deaths did occur: Sir Nicholas de Mimsy-Porpington (a wizard at the Royal Court in his lifetime, and in his death-time, ghost of Gryffindor Tower) was stripped of his wand before being locked in a dungeon, and was unable to magic himself out of his execution; and Wizarding families were particularly prone to losing younger members, whose inability to control their own magic made them noticeable, and vulnerable, to Muggle witch-hunters.

"Let the Muggles manage without us!" was the cry, as wizards drew further and further apart from their non-magical brethren, culminating with the institution of the International Statute of Wizarding Secrecy in 1689, when wizardkind voluntarily went underground.

Children being children, however, the grotesque Hopping Pot had taken hold of their imaginations. The solution was to jettison the pro-Muggle moral but keep the warty cauldron, so by the middle of the sixteenth century a different version of the tale was in wide circulation among Wizarding families. In the revised story, the Hopping Pot protects an innocent wizard from his torch-bearing, pitchfork-toting neighbors by chasing them away from the wizard's cottage, catching them, and swallowing them whole. At the end of the story, by which time the Pot has consumed most of his neighbors, the wizard gains a promise from the few remaining villagers that he will be left in peace to practice magic. In return, he instructs the Pot to render up its victims, who are duly burped out of its depths, slightly mangled. To this day, some Wizarding children are only told the revised version of the story by their (generally anti-Muggle) parents, and the original, if and when they ever read it, comes as a great surprise.

As I have already hinted, however, its pro-Muggle sentiment was not the only reason

that "The Wizard and the Hopping Pot"
attracted anger. As the witch hunts grew ever
fiercer, Wizarding families began to live double
lives, using charms of concealment to protect
themselves and their families. By the seven-
teenth century, any witch or wizard who chose
to fraternize with Muggles became suspect,
even an outcast in his or her own community.
Among the many insults hurled at pro-Muggle
witches and wizards (such fruity epithets as
"Mudwallower," "Dunglicker," and "Scum-
sucker" date from this period) was the charge of
having weak or inferior magic.

Influential wizards of the day such as
Brutus Malfoy, editor of *Warlock at War,*
an anti-Muggle periodical, perpetuated the

stereotype that a Muggle-lover was about as magical as a Squib.[2] In 1675, Brutus wrote:

> *This we may state with certainty: Any wizard who shows fondness for the society of Muggles is of low intelligence, with magic so feeble and pitiful that he can only feel himself superior if surrounded by Muggle pig-men.*
>
> *Nothing is a surer sign of weak magic than a weakness for non-magical company.*

This prejudice eventually died out in the face of overwhelming evidence that some of the

---

2 [A Squib is a person born to magical parents, but who has no magical powers. Such an occurrence is rare. Muggle-born witches and wizards are much more common. — JKR]

world's most brilliant wizards[3] were, to use the common phrase, "Muggle-lovers."

The final objection to "The Wizard and the Hopping Pot" remains alive in certain quarters today. It was summed up best, perhaps, by Beatrix Bloxam (1794–1910), author of the infamous *Toadstool Tales*. Mrs. Bloxam believed that *The Tales of Beedle the Bard* were damaging to children, because of what she called "their unhealthy preoccupation with the most horrid subjects, such as death, disease, bloodshed, wicked magic, unwholesome characters, and bodily effusions and eruptions of the most disgusting kind." Mrs. Bloxam took a variety of old stories, including several of Beedle's, and rewrote them

---

3 Such as myself.

according to her ideals, which she expressed as "filling the pure minds of our little angels with healthy, happy thoughts, keeping their sweet slumber free of wicked dreams, and protecting the precious flower of their innocence."

The final paragraph of Mrs. Bloxam's pure and precious reworking of "The Wizard and the Hopping Pot" reads:

> *Then the little golden pot danced with delight — hoppitty hoppitty hop! — on its tiny rosy toes! Wee Willykins had cured all the dollies of their poorly tum-tums, and the little pot was so happy that it filled up with*

*sweeties for Wee Willykins and the*

*dollies!*

*"But don't forget to brush your*

*teethy-pegs!" cried the pot.*

*And Wee Willykins kissed and*

*huggled the hoppitty pot and promised*

*always to help the dollies and never to*

*be an old grumpy-wumpkins again.*

Mrs. Bloxam's tale has met the same
response from generations of Wizarding children:
uncontrollable retching, followed by an imme-
diate demand to have the book taken from them
and mashed into pulp.

# THE FOUNTAIN OF
# FAIR FORTUNE

High on a hill in an enchanted garden, enclosed by tall walls and protected by strong magic, flowed the Fountain of Fair Fortune.

Once a year, between the hours of sunrise and sunset on the longest day, a single unfortunate was given the chance to fight their way to the Fountain, bathe in its waters, and receive Fair Fortune forevermore.

On the appointed day, hundreds of people

traveled from all over the kingdom to reach the garden walls before dawn. Male and female, rich and poor, young and old, of magical means and without, they gathered in the darkness, each hoping that they would be the one to gain entrance to the garden.

Three witches, each with her burden of woe, met on the outskirts of the crowd, and told one another their sorrows as they waited for sunrise.

The first, by name Asha, was sick of a malady no Healer could cure. She hoped that the Fountain would banish her symptoms and grant her a long and happy life.

The second, by name Altheda, had been robbed of her home, her gold, and her wand by an evil sorcerer. She hoped that the Fountain might relieve her of powerlessness and poverty.

The third, by name Amata, had been deserted by a man whom she loved dearly, and she thought her heart would never mend. She hoped that the Fountain would relieve her of her grief and longing.

Pitying each other, the three women agreed that, should the chance befall them, they would unite and try to reach the Fountain together.

The sky was rent with the first ray of sun, and a chink in the wall opened. The crowd surged forward, each of them shrieking their claim for the Fountain's benison. Creepers from the garden beyond snaked through the pressing mass, and twisted themselves around the first witch, Asha. She grasped the wrist of the second witch, Altheda, who seized tight upon the robes of the third witch, Amata.

And Amata became caught upon the armor of a dismal-looking knight, who was seated on a bone-thin horse.

The creepers tugged the three witches through the chink in the wall, and the knight was dragged off his steed after them.

The furious screams of the disappointed throng rose upon the morning air, then fell silent as the garden walls sealed once more.

Asha and Altheda were angry with Amata, who had accidentally brought along the knight.

"Only one can bathe in the Fountain! It will be hard enough to decide which of us it will be, without adding another!"

Now, Sir Luckless, as the knight was known in the land outside the walls, observed that these were witches, and, having no magic, nor any great skill at jousting or dueling with swords, nor anything that distinguished the non-magical man, was sure that he had no hope of beating the three women to the Fountain. He therefore declared his intention of withdrawing outside the walls again.

At this, Amata became angry too.

"Faint heart!" she chided him. "Draw your sword, Knight, and help us reach our goal!"

And so the three witches and the forlorn

knight ventured forth into the enchanted

garden, where rare herbs, fruit, and flowers grew

in abundance on either side of the sunlit paths. They met no obstacle until they reached the foot of the hill on which the Fountain stood.

There, however, wrapped around the base of the hill, was a monstrous white Worm, bloated and blind. At their approach it turned a foul face upon them, and uttered the following words:

"Pay me the proof of your pain."

Sir Luckless drew his sword and attempted to kill the beast, but his blade snapped. Then Altheda cast rocks at the Worm, while Asha and Amata essayed every spell that might subdue or entrance it, but the power of their wands was no more effective than their friend's stones or the knight's steel: The Worm would not let them pass.

The sun rose higher and higher in the sky, and Asha, despairing, began to weep.

Then the great Worm placed its face upon hers and drank the tears from her cheeks. Its thirst assuaged, the Worm slithered aside, and vanished into a hole in the ground.

Rejoicing at the Worm's disappearance, the three witches and the knight began to climb the hill, sure that they would reach the Fountain before noon.

Halfway up the steep slope, however, they came across words cut into the ground before them:

"Pay me the fruit of your labors."

Sir Luckless took out his only coin, and placed it upon the grassy hillside, but it rolled away and was lost. The three witches and the knight continued to climb, but though they walked for hours more, they advanced not a step; the summit came no nearer, and still the inscription lay in the earth before them.

All were discouraged as the sun rose over their heads and began to sink toward the far horizon, but Altheda walked faster and harder than any of them, and exhorted the others to follow her example, though she moved no farther up the enchanted hill.

"Courage, friends, and do not yield!" she cried, wiping the sweat from her brow.

As the drops fell glittering onto the earth, the inscription blocking their path vanished, and they found that they were able to move upward once more.

Delighted by the removal of this second obstacle, they hurried toward the summit as fast as they could, until at last they glimpsed the Fountain, glittering like crystal in a bower of flowers and trees.

Before they could reach it, however, they came to a stream that ran around the hilltop, barring their way. In the depths of the clear water lay a smooth stone bearing the words:

"Pay me the treasure of your past."

Sir Luckless attempted to float across the stream on his shield, but it sank. The three witches pulled him from the water, then tried to

leap the brook themselves, but it would not let

them cross, and all the while the sun was sinking

lower in the sky.

So they fell to pondering the meaning of

the stone's message, and Amata was the first to

understand. Taking her wand, she drew from

her mind all the memories of happy times she

had spent with her vanished lover, and dropped

them into the rushing waters. The stream swept

them away, and stepping stones appeared, and

the three witches and the knight were able to

pass at last onto the summit of the hill.

The Fountain shimmered before them, set

amidst herbs and flowers rarer and more beauti-

ful than any they had yet seen. The sky burned

ruby, and it was time to decide which of them would bathe.

Before they could make their decision, however, frail Asha fell to the ground. Exhausted by their struggle to the summit, she was close to death.

Her three friends would have carried her to the Fountain, but Asha was in mortal agony and begged them not to touch her.

Then Altheda hastened to pick all those herbs she thought most hopeful, and mixed them in Sir Luckless's gourd of water, and poured the potion into Asha's mouth.

At once, Asha was able to stand. What was more, all symptoms of her dread malady had vanished.

"I am cured!" she cried. "I have no need of the Fountain — let Altheda bathe!"

But Altheda was busy collecting more herbs in her apron.

"If I can cure this disease, I shall earn gold aplenty! Let Amata bathe!"

Sir Luckless bowed and gestured Amata toward the Fountain, but she shook her head. The stream had washed away all regret for her lover, and she saw now that he had been cruel and faithless, and that it was happiness enough to be rid of him.

"Good sir, you must bathe, as a reward for all your chivalry!" she told Sir Luckless.

So the knight clanked forth in the last rays of

the setting sun, and bathed in the Fountain of Fair Fortune, astonished that he was the chosen one of hundreds and giddy with his incredible luck.

As the sun fell below the horizon, Sir Luckless emerged from the waters with the glory of his triumph upon him, and flung himself in his rusted armor at the feet of Amata, who was the kindest and most beautiful woman he had ever beheld. Flushed with success, he begged for her hand and her heart, and Amata, no less delighted, realized that she had found a man worthy of them.

The three witches and the knight set off down the hill together, arm in arm, and all four led long and happy lives, and none of them ever

knew or suspected that the Fountain's waters

carried no enchantment at all.

# ALBUS DUMBLEDORE

## on *"The Fountain of Fair Fortune"*

"The Fountain of Fair Fortune" is a perennial favorite, so much so that it was the subject of the sole attempt to introduce a Christmas pantomime[1] to Hogwarts's festive celebrations.

Our then Herbology master, Professor Herbert Beery,[2] an enthusiastic devotee of amateur dramatics, proposed an adaptation of this well-beloved children's tale as a Yuletide

---

1 [Non-British Muggles may be unfamiliar with the British tradition of plays presented at Christmastime, usually based on fairy tales and including music, comical characters, and audience participation (though not, generally, of the vigorous type described here). — JKR]

2 Professor Beery eventually left Hogwarts to teach at W.A.D.A. (Wizarding Academy of Dramatic Arts), where, he once confessed to me, he maintained a strong aversion to mounting performances of this particular story, believing it to be unlucky.

treat for staff and students. I was then a young Transfiguration teacher, and Herbert assigned me to "special effects," which included providing a fully functioning Fountain of Fair Fortune and a miniature grassy hill, up which our three heroines and hero would appear to march, while it sank slowly into the stage and out of sight.

I think I may say, without vanity, that both my Fountain and my Hill performed the parts allotted to them with simple goodwill. Alas, that the same could not be said of the rest of the cast. Ignoring for a moment the antics of the gigantic "worm" provided by our Care of Magical Creatures teacher, Professor Silvanus Kettleburn, the human element proved disastrous to the show. Professor Beery, in his role of director, had been dangerously oblivious to the emotional entanglements seething under his very nose. Little did he know that the students playing "Amata" and "Sir Luckless" had been boyfriend and girlfriend until one hour before the curtain rose, at which point "Sir Luckless" transferred his affections to "Asha."

Suffice it to say that our seekers after Fair Fortune never made it to the top of the hill. The curtain had barely risen when Professor Kettleburn's "worm" — now revealed to be an Ashwinder[3] with an Engorgement Charm upon

_____

3 See *Fantastic Beasts and Where to Find Them* for a definitive description of this curious beast. It ought never to be voluntarily introduced into a wood-paneled room, nor have an Engorgement Charm placed upon it.

it — exploded in a shower of hot sparks and dust, filling the Great Hall with smoke and fragments of scenery. While the enormous fiery eggs it had laid at the foot of my Hill ignited the floorboards, "Amata" and "Asha" turned upon each other, dueling so fiercely that Professor Beery was caught in the cross fire, and the staff had to evacuate the Hall, as the inferno now raging onstage threatened to engulf the place. The night's entertainment concluded with a packed hospital wing; it was several months before the Great Hall lost its pungent aroma of wood smoke, and even longer before Professor Beery's head reassumed its normal proportions, and Professor Kettleburn was taken off probation.[4] Headmaster Armando Dippet imposed a blanket ban on future pantomimes, a proud non-theatrical tradition that Hogwarts continues to this day.

Our dramatic fiasco notwithstanding, "The Fountain of Fair Fortune" is probably the most popular of Beedle's tales, although, just like "The Wizard and the Hopping Pot," it has its detractors. More than one parent has demanded the removal of this particular tale from

---

4 Professor Kettleburn survived no fewer than sixty-two periods of probation during his employment as Care of Magical Creatures teacher. His relations with my predecessor at Hogwarts, Professor Dippet, were always strained, Professor Dippet considering him to be somewhat reckless. By the time I became headmaster, however, Professor Kettleburn had mellowed considerably, although there were always those who took the cynical view that with only one and a half of his original limbs remaining to him, he was forced to take life at a quieter pace.

the Hogwarts library, including, by coincidence, a descendant of Brutus Malfoy and one-time member of the Hogwarts Board of Governors, Mr. Lucius Malfoy. Mr. Malfoy submitted his demand for a ban on the story in writing:

> *Any work of fiction or nonfiction that depicts interbreeding between wizards and Muggles should be banned from the bookshelves of Hogwarts. I do not wish my son to be influenced into sullying the purity of his bloodline by reading stories that promote wizard–Muggle marriage.*

My refusal to remove the book from the library was backed by a majority of the Board of Governors. I wrote back to Mr. Malfoy, explaining my decision:

> *So-called pure-blood families*
> *maintain their alleged purity by*
> *disowning, banishing, or lying about*
> *Muggles or Muggle-borns on their*
> *family trees. They then attempt to*
> *foist their hypocrisy upon the rest of*
> *us by asking us to ban works dealing*
> *with the truths they deny. There is*
> *not a witch or wizard in existence*
> *whose blood has not mingled with*
> *that of Muggles, and I should there-*
> *fore consider it both illogical and*
> *immoral to remove works dealing*

*with the subject from our students'*

*store of knowledge.*[5]

This exchange marked the beginning of Mr. Malfoy's long campaign to have me removed from my post as headmaster of Hogwarts, and of mine to have him removed from his position as Lord Voldemort's Favorite Death Eater.

---

5 My response prompted several further letters from Mr. Malfoy, but as they consisted mainly of opprobrious remarks on my sanity, parentage, and hygiene, their relevance to this commentary is remote.

# THE WARLOCK'S
# HAIRY HEART

There was once a handsome, rich, and talented young warlock, who observed that his friends grew foolish when they fell in love, gamboling and preening, losing their appetites and their dignity. The young warlock resolved never to fall prey to such weakness, and employed Dark Arts to ensure his immunity.

Unaware of his secret, the warlock's family laughed to see him so aloof and cold.

"All will change," they prophesied, "when a maid catches his fancy!"

But the young warlock's fancy remained untouched. Though many a maiden was intrigued by his haughty mien, and employed her most subtle arts to please him, none succeeded in touching his heart. The warlock gloried in his indifference, and the sagacity that had produced it.

The first freshness of youth waned, and the warlock's peers began to wed, and then to bring forth children.

"Their hearts must be husks," he sneered inwardly as he observed the antics of the young parents around him, "shriveled by the demands of these mewling offspring!"

And once again he congratulated himself upon the wisdom of his early choice.

In due course, the warlock's aged parents died. Their son did not mourn them; on the contrary, he considered himself blessed by their demise. Now he reigned alone in their castle. Having transferred his greatest treasure to the deepest dungeon, he gave himself over to a life of ease and plenty, his comfort the only aim of his many servants.

The warlock was sure that he must be an object of immense envy to all who beheld his splendid and untroubled solitude. Fierce were his anger and chagrin, therefore, when he overheard two of his lackeys discussing their master one day.

The first servant expressed pity for the warlock who, with all his wealth and power, was yet beloved by nobody.

But his companion jeered, asking why a man with so much gold and a palatial castle to his name had been unable to attract a wife.

Their words dealt dreadful blows to the listening warlock's pride. He resolved at once to take a wife, and that she would be a wife superior to all others. She would possess astounding beauty, exciting envy and desire in every man who beheld her; she would spring from magical lineage, so that their offspring would inherit outstanding magical gifts; and she would have wealth at least equal to his own, so that his comfortable existence would be assured, in spite of additions to his household.

It might have taken the warlock fifty years to find such a woman, yet it so happened that the very day after he decided to seek her, a maiden answering his every wish arrived in the neighborhood to visit her kinsfolk.

She was a witch of prodigious skill and possessed of much gold. Her beauty was such that it tugged at the heart of every man who set eyes on her; of every man, that is, except one. The warlock's heart felt nothing at all. Nevertheless, she was the prize he sought, so he began to pay her court.

All who noticed the warlock's change in manners were amazed, and told the maiden that she had succeeded where a hundred had failed.

The young woman herself was both fasci- nated and repelled by the warlock's attentions. She sensed the coldness that lay behind the warmth of his flattery, and had never met a man so strange and remote. Her kinsfolk, however, deemed theirs a most suitable match, and, eager to promote it, accepted the warlock's invitation to a great feast in the maiden's honor.

The table was laden with silver and gold, bearing the finest wines and most sumptuous foods. Minstrels strummed on silk-stringed lutes and sang of a love their master had never felt. The maiden sat upon a throne beside the warlock, who spake low, employing words of tenderness he had stolen from the poets, without any idea of their true meaning.

The maiden listened, puzzled, and finally replied, "You speak well, Warlock, and I would be delighted by your attentions, if only I thought you had a heart!"

The warlock smiled, and told her that she need not fear on that score. Bidding her follow, he led her from the feast, and down to the locked dungeon where he kept his greatest treasure.

Here, in an enchanted crystal casket, was the warlock's beating heart.

Long since disconnected from eyes, ears, and fingers, it had never fallen prey to beauty, or to a musical voice, to the feel of silken skin. The maiden was terrified by the sight of it, for the heart was shrunken and covered in long black hair.

"Oh, what have you done?" she lamented. "Put it back where it belongs, I beseech you!"

Seeing that this was necessary to please her, the warlock drew his wand, unlocked the crystal casket, sliced open his own breast, and replaced the hairy heart in the empty cavity it had once occupied.

"Now you are healed and will know true love!" cried the maiden, and she embraced him.

The touch of her soft white arms, the sound of her breath in his ear, the scent of her heavy gold hair: All pierced the newly awakened heart like spears. But it had grown strange during its long exile, blind and savage in the darkness to which it had been condemned, and its appetites had grown powerful and perverse.

The guests at the feast had noticed the absence of their host and the maiden. At first untroubled, they grew anxious as the hours passed, and finally began to search the castle.

They found the dungeon at last, and a most dreadful sight awaited them there.

The maiden lay dead upon the floor, her breast cut open, and beside her crouched the mad warlock, holding in one bloody hand a great, smooth, shining scarlet heart, which he licked and stroked, vowing to exchange it for his own.

In his other hand, he held his wand, trying to coax from his own chest the shriveled, hairy heart. But the hairy heart was stronger than he was, and refused to relinquish its hold upon his senses or to return to the coffin in which it had been locked for so long.

Before the horror-struck eyes of his guests, the warlock cast aside his wand, and seized a silver dagger. Vowing never to be mastered by his own heart, he hacked it from his chest.

For one moment, the warlock knelt triumphant, with a heart clutched in each hand; then he fell across the maiden's body, and died.

# ALBUS DUMBLEDORE

## on *"The Warlock's Hairy Heart"*

As we have already seen, Beedle's first two tales
attracted criticism of their themes of generos-
ity, tolerance, and love. "The Warlock's Hairy
Heart," however, does not appear to have been
modified or much criticized in the hundreds
of years since it was first written; the story as
I eventually read it in the original runes was
almost exactly that which my mother had told
me. That said, "The Warlock's Hairy Heart" is
by far the most gruesome of Beedle's offerings,
and many parents do not share it with their

children until they think they are old enough
not to suffer nightmares.[1]

Why, then, the survival of this grisly tale?
I would argue that "The Warlock's Hairy
Heart" has survived intact through the centuries because it speaks to the dark depths in all
of us. It addresses one of the greatest, and least

---

1 According to her own diary, Beatrix Bloxam never recovered from
overhearing this story being told by her aunt to her older cousins. "Quite
by accident, my little ear fell against the keyhole. I can only imagine
that I must have been paralyzed with horror, for I inadvertently heard
the whole of the disgusting story, not to mention ghastly details of the
dreadfully unsavory affair of my Uncle Nobby, the local hag, and a sack
of Bouncing Bulbs. The shock almost killed me; I was in bed for a week,
and so deeply traumatized was I that I developed the habit of sleep-
walking back to the same keyhole every night, until at last my dear Papa,
with only my best interests at heart, put a Sticking Charm on my door at
bedtime." Apparently Beatrix could find no way to make "The Warlock's
Hairy Heart" suitable for children's sensitive ears, as she never rewrote it
for *The Toadstool Tales*.

acknowledged, temptations of magic: the quest for invulnerability.

Of course, such a quest is nothing more or less than a foolish fantasy. No man or woman alive, magical or not, has ever escaped some form of injury, whether physical, mental, or emotional. To hurt is as human as to breathe. Nevertheless, we wizards seem particularly prone to the idea that we can bend the nature of existence to our will. The young warlock[2] in this

2 [The term "warlock" is a very old one. Although it is sometimes used as interchangeable with "wizard," it originally denoted one learned in dueling and all martial magic. It was also given as a title to wizards who had performed feats of bravery, rather as Muggles were sometimes knighted for acts of valor. By calling the young wizard in this story a warlock, Beedle indicates that he has already been recognized as especially skillful at offensive magic. These days wizards use "warlock" in one of two ways: to describe a wizard of unusually fierce appearance, or as a title denoting particular skill or achievement. Thus, Dumbledore himself was Chief Warlock of the Wizengamot. — JKR]

story, for instance, decides that falling in love would adversely affect his comfort and security. He sees love as a humiliation, a weakness, a drain on a person's emotional and material resources.

Of course, the centuries-old trade in love potions shows that our fictional wizard is hardly alone in seeking to control the unpredictable course of love. The search for a true love potion[3] continues to this day, but no such elixir has yet been created, and leading potioneers doubt that it is possible.

---

3 Hector Dagworth-Granger, founder of the Most Extraordinary Society of Potioneers, explains: "Powerful infatuations can be induced by the skillful potioneer, but never yet has anyone managed to create the truly unbreakable, eternal, unconditional attachment that alone can be called Love."

The hero in this tale, however, is not even interested in a simulacrum of love that he can create or destroy at will. He wants to remain forever uninfected by what he regards as a kind of sickness, and therefore performs a piece of Dark Magic that would not be possible outside of a storybook: He locks away his own heart.

The resemblance of this action to the creation of a Horcrux has been noted by many writers. Although Beedle's hero is not seeking to avoid death, he is dividing what was clearly not meant to be divided — body and heart, rather than soul — and in doing so, he is falling foul of the first of Adalbert Waffling's Fundamental Laws of Magic:

*Tamper with the deepest mysteries —*
*the source of life, the essence of self —*
*only if prepared for consequences of*
*the most extreme and dangerous kind.*

And sure enough, in seeking to become superhuman this foolhardy young man renders himself inhuman. The heart he has locked away slowly shrivels and grows hair, symbolizing his own descent to beasthood. He is finally reduced to a violent animal who takes what he wants by force, and he dies in a futile attempt to regain what is now forever beyond his reach — a human heart.

Though somewhat dated, the expression

"to have a hairy heart" has passed into everyday Wizarding language to describe a cold or unfeeling witch or wizard. My maiden aunt Honoria always alleged that she called off her engagement to a wizard in the Improper Use of Magic Office because she discovered in time that "he had a hairy heart." (It was rumored, however, that she actually discovered him in the act of fondling some Horklumps,[4] which she found deeply shocking.) More recently, the self-help book *The Hairy Heart: A Guide to Wizards Who Won't Commit*[5] has topped bestseller lists.

---

4 Horklumps are pink, bristly mushroom-like creatures. It is very difficult to see why anyone would want to fondle them. For further information, see *Fantastic Beasts and Where to Find Them*.
5 Not to be confused with *Hairy Snout, Human Heart,* a heartrending account of one man's struggle with lycanthropy.

# BABBITTY RABBITTY AND HER CACKLING STUMP

A long time ago, in a far-off land, there lived a foolish King who decided that he alone should have the power of magic.

He therefore commanded the head of his army to form a Brigade of Witch-Hunters, and issued them a pack of ferocious black hounds. At the same time, the King caused proclamations to be read in every village and town across the land: "Wanted by the King: an Instructor in Magic."

No true witch or wizard dared volunteer for the post, for they were all in hiding from the Brigade of Witch-Hunters.

However, a cunning charlatan with no magical power saw a chance of enriching himself, and arrived at the palace, claiming to be a wizard of enormous skill. The charlatan performed a few simple tricks that convinced the foolish King of his magical powers, and was immediately appointed Grand Sorcerer in Chief, the King's Private Magic Master.

The charlatan bade the King give him a large sack of gold, so that he might purchase wands and other magical necessities. He also requested several large rubies, to be used in the casting of curative charms, and a silver chalice

or two, for the storing and maturing of potions.
All these things the foolish King supplied.

The charlatan stowed the treasure safely
in his own house and returned to the palace
grounds.

He did not know that he was being watched
by an old woman who lived in a hovel on the
edge of the grounds. Her name was Babbitty,
and she was the washerwoman who kept the
palace linens soft, fragrant, and white. Peeping
from behind her drying sheets, Babbitty saw the
charlatan snap two twigs from one of the King's
trees, and disappear into the palace.

The charlatan gave one of the twigs to the
King and assured him that it was a wand of
tremendous power.

"It will only work, however," said the charlatan, "when you are worthy of it."

Every morning the charlatan and the foolish King walked out into the palace grounds, where they waved their wands and shouted nonsense at the sky. The charlatan was careful to perform more tricks, so that the King remained convinced of his Grand Sorcerer's skill, and of the power of the wands that had cost so much gold.

One morning, as the charlatan and the foolish King were twirling their twigs, and hopping in circles, and chanting meaningless rhymes, a loud cackling reached the King's ears. Babbitty the washerwoman was watching the King and the charlatan from the window of her tiny cottage, and was laughing so hard she soon sank out of sight, too weak to stand.

"I must look most undignified, to make the old washerwoman laugh so!" said the King. He ceased his hopping and twig-twirling, and frowned. "I grow weary of practice! When shall I be ready to perform real spells in front of my subjects, Sorcerer?"

The charlatan tried to soothe his pupil, assuring him that he would soon be capable of astonishing feats of magic, but Babbitty's cackling had stung the foolish King more than the charlatan knew.

"Tomorrow," said the King, "we shall invite our court to watch their King perform magic!"

The charlatan saw that the time had come to take his treasure and flee.

"Alas, Your Majesty, it is impossible! I had forgotten to tell Your Majesty that I must set out on a long journey tomorrow —"

"If you leave this palace without my permission, Sorcerer, my Brigade of Witch-Hunters will hunt you down with their hounds! Tomorrow morning you will assist me to perform magic for the benefit of my Lords and Ladies, and if anybody laughs at me, I shall have you beheaded!"

The King stormed back to the palace, leaving the charlatan alone and afraid. Not all his cunning could save him now, for he could not

run away, nor could he help the King with
magic that neither of them knew.

Seeking a vent for his fear and his anger, the
charlatan approached the window of Babbitty
the washerwoman. Peering inside, he saw the
little old lady sitting at her table, polishing a
wand. In a corner behind her, the King's sheets
were washing themselves in a wooden tub.

The charlatan understood at once that
Babbitty was a true witch, and that she who had
given him his awful problem could also solve it.

"Crone!" roared the charlatan. "Your cackling has cost me dear! If you fail to help me, I
shall denounce you as a witch, and it will be you
who is torn apart by the King's hounds!"

Old Babbitty smiled at the charlatan, and assured him that she would do everything in her power to help.

The charlatan instructed her to conceal herself inside a bush while the King gave his magical display, and to perform the King's spells for him without his knowledge. Babbitty agreed to the plan, but asked one question.

"What, sir, if the King attempts a spell Babbitty cannot perform?"

The charlatan scoffed.

"Your magic is more than equal to that fool's imagination," he assured her, and he retired to the castle, well pleased with his own cleverness.

The following morning all the Lords and

Ladies of the kingdom assembled in the palace grounds. The King climbed onto a stage in front of them, with the charlatan by his side.

"I shall firstly make this Lady's hat disappear!" cried the King, pointing his twig at a noblewoman.

From inside a bush nearby, Babbitty pointed her wand at the hat, and caused it to vanish. Great was the astonishment and admiration of the crowd, and loud their applause for the jubilant King.

"Next, I shall make that horse fly!" cried the King, pointing his twig at his own steed.

From inside the bush, Babbitty pointed her wand at the horse and it rose high into the air.

# THE TALES OF
# BEEDLE THE BARD

The crowd was still more thrilled and amazed, and they roared their appreciation of their magical King.

"And now," said the King, looking all around for an idea; and the Captain of his Brigade of Witch-Hunters ran forward.

"Your Majesty," said the Captain, "this very morning, Sabre died of eating a poisonous toadstool! Bring him back to life, Your Majesty, with your wand!"

And the Captain heaved onto the stage the lifeless body of the largest of the witch-hunting hounds.

The foolish King brandished his twig and pointed it at the dead dog. But inside the bush,

Babbitty smiled and did not trouble to lift her
wand, for no magic can raise the dead.

When the dog did not stir, the crowd began
first to whisper, and then to laugh. They suspected that the King's first two feats had been
mere tricks after all.

"Why doesn't it work?" the King screamed
at the charlatan, who bethought himself of the
only ruse left to him.

"There, Your Majesty, there!" he shouted,
pointing at the bush where Babbitty sat con-
cealed. "I see her plain, a wicked witch who is
blocking your magic with her own evil spells!
Seize her, somebody, seize her!"

Babbitty fled from the bush, and the Brigade
of Witch-Hunters set off in pursuit, unleashing

their hounds, who bayed for Babbitty's blood.
But as she reached a low hedge, the little witch
vanished from sight, and when the King, the
charlatan, and all the courtiers gained the other
side, they found the pack of witch-hunting
hounds barking and scrabbling around a bent
and aged tree.

"She has turned herself into a tree!" screamed
the charlatan, and, dreading lest Babbitty turn
back into a woman and denounce him, he
added, "Cut her down, Your Majesty, that is
the way to treat evil witches!"

An axe was brought at once, and the old tree
was felled to loud cheers from the courtiers and
the charlatan.

However, as they were making ready to

return to the palace, the sound of loud cackling stopped them in their tracks.

"Fools!" cried Babbitty's voice from the stump they had left behind.

"No witch or wizard can be killed by being cut in half! Take the axe, if you do not believe me, and cut the Grand Sorcerer in two!"

The Captain of the Brigade of Witch-Hunters was eager to make the experiment, but as he raised the axe the charlatan fell to his knees, screaming for mercy and confessing all his wickedness. As he was dragged away to the dungeons, the tree stump cackled more loudly than ever.

"By cutting a witch in half, you have un-leashed a dreadful curse upon your kingdom!"

it told the petrified King. "Henceforth, every stroke of harm that you inflict upon my fellow witches and wizards will feel like an axe stroke in your own side, until you will wish you could die of it!"

At that, the King fell to his knees too, and told the stump that he would issue a proclamation at once, protecting all the witches and wizards of the kingdom, and allowing them to practice their magic in peace.

"Very good," said the stump, "but you have not yet made amends to Babbitty!"

"Anything, anything at all!" cried the foolish King, wringing his hands before the stump.

"You will erect a statue of Babbitty upon me, in memory of your poor washerwoman, and

to remind you forever of your own foolishness!"
said the stump.

The King agreed to it at once, and promised
to engage the foremost sculptor in the land, and
have the statue made of pure gold. Then the
shamed King and all the noblemen and -women
returned to the palace, leaving the tree stump
cackling behind them.

When the grounds were deserted once
more, there wriggled from a hole between the
roots of the tree stump a stout and whiskery
old rabbit with a wand clamped between her
teeth. Babbitty hopped out of the grounds and
far away, and ever after a golden statue of the
washerwoman stood upon the tree stump, and

no witch or wizard was ever persecuted in the kingdom again.

# ALBUS DUMBLEDORE

*on "Babbitty Rabbitty and
Her Cackling Stump"*

The story of "Babbitty Rabbitty and Her Cackling Stump" is, in many ways, the most "real" of Beedle's tales, in that the magic described in the story conforms, almost entirely, to known magical laws.

It was through this story that many of us first discovered that magic could not bring back the dead — and a great disappointment and shock it was, convinced as we had been, as young children, that our parents would be able to awaken our dead rats and cats with one wave of their wands. Though some six centuries have elapsed since Beedle wrote this tale, and while we have devised innumerable ways of maintaining the illusion of our loved ones' continuing presence,[1] wizards still have not found a way of reuniting body and soul once death has occurred. As the eminent Wizarding philosopher Bertrand de Pensées-Profondes writes in his celebrated work *A Study into the Possibility of Reversing the Actual and Metaphysical Effects of Natural Death, with*

---

1 [Wizarding photographs and portraits move and (in the case of the latter) talk just like their subjects. Other rare objects, such as the Mirror of Erised, may also reveal more than a static image of a lost loved one. Ghosts are transparent, moving, talking, and thinking versions of wizards and witches who wished, for whatever reason, to remain on earth. — JKR]

*Particular Regard to the Reintegration of Essence*
*and Matter:*

> *"Give it up. It's never going to*
> *happen."*

The tale of Babbitty Rabbitty does, however, give us one of the earliest literary mentions of an Animagus, for Babbitty the washerwoman is possessed of the rare magical ability to transform into an animal at will.

Animagi make up a small fraction of the Wizarding population. Achieving perfect, spontaneous human-to-animal transformation requires much study and practice, and many witches and wizards consider that their time might be better employed in other ways.

Certainly the application of such a talent is limited unless one has a great need of disguise or concealment. It is for this reason that the Ministry of Magic has insisted upon a register of Animagi, for there can be no doubt that this kind of magic is of greatest use to those engaged in surreptitious, covert, or even criminal activity.[2]

Whether there was ever a washerwoman who was able to transform into a rabbit is open to doubt; however, some magical historians have suggested that Beedle modeled Babbitty on the famous French sorceress Lisette de Lapin, who

---

2 [Professor McGonagall, Headmistress of Hogwarts, has asked me to make clear that she became an Animagus merely as a result of her extensive researches into all fields of Transfiguration, and that she has never used the ability to turn into a tabby cat for any surreptitious purpose, setting aside legitimate business on behalf of the Order of the Phoenix, where secrecy and concealment were imperative. — JKR]

was convicted of witchcraft in Paris in 1422. To the astonishment of her Muggle guards, who were later tried for helping the witch to escape, Lisette vanished from her prison cell the night before she was due to be executed. Although it has never been proven that Lisette was an Animagus who managed to squeeze through the bars of her cell window, a large white rabbit was subsequently seen crossing the English Channel in a cauldron with a sail fitted to it, and a similar rabbit later became a trusted advisor at the court of King Henry VI.[3]

The King in Beedle's story is a foolish Muggle who both covets and fears magic. He

---

[3] This may have contributed to that Muggle King's reputation for mental instability.

believes that he can become a wizard simply by learning incantations and waving a wand.[4] He is completely ignorant of the true nature of magic and wizards, and therefore swallows the preposterous suggestions of both the charlatan and Babbitty. This is certainly typical of a particular type of Muggle thinking: In their ignorance, they are prepared to accept all sorts of impossibilities about magic, including the proposition that Babbitty has turned herself

---

4 As intensive studies in the Department of Mysteries demonstrated as far back as 1672, wizards and witches are born, not created. While the "rogue" ability to perform magic sometimes appears in those of apparent non-magical descent (though several later studies have suggested that there will have been a witch or wizard somewhere on the family tree), Muggles cannot perform magic. The best — or worst — they could hope for are random and uncontrollable effects generated by a genuine magical wand, which, as an instrument through which magic is supposed to be channeled, sometimes holds residual power, which it may discharge at odd moments — see also the notes on wandlore for "The Tale of the Three Brothers."

into a tree that can still think and talk. (It is worth noting at this point, however, that while Beedle uses the talking-tree device to show us how ignorant the Muggle King is, he also asks us to believe that Babbitty can talk while she is a rabbit. This might be poetic license, but I think it more likely that Beedle had only heard about Animagi, and never met one, for this is the only liberty that he takes with magical laws in the story. Animagi do not retain the power of human speech while in their animal form, although they keep all their human thinking and reasoning powers. This, as every schoolchild knows, is the fundamental difference between being an Animagus and Transfiguring oneself into an animal. In the case of the latter, one would become the animal entirely, with the consequence that one would know no magic, be unaware that one had ever been a wizard, and would need somebody else to Transfigure one back to one's original form.)

I think it possible that in choosing to make his heroine pretend to turn into a tree, and threaten the King with pain like an axe stroke in his own side, Beedle was inspired by real magical traditions and practices. Trees with wand-quality wood have always been fiercely protected by the wandmakers who tend them, and cutting down such trees to steal them risks incurring not only the malice of the Bowtruckles[5] usually

---

5 For a full description of these curious little tree-dwellers, see *Fantastic Beasts and Where to Find Them.*

nesting there, but also the ill effects of protective curses placed around them by their owners. In Beedle's time, the Cruciatus Curse had not yet been made illegal by the Ministry of Magic,[6] and could have produced precisely the sensation with which Babbitty threatens the King.

---

6 The Cruciatus, Imperius, and Avada Kedavra curses were first classified as Unforgivable in 1717, with the strictest penalties attached to their use.

# THE TALE OF THE
# THREE BROTHERS

There were once three brothers who were traveling along a lonely, winding road at twilight. In time, the brothers reached a river too deep to wade through and too dangerous to swim across. However, these brothers were learned in the magical arts, and so they simply waved their wands and made a bridge appear across the treacherous water. They were halfway across it when they found their path blocked by a hooded figure.

And Death spoke to them. He was angry that he had been cheated out of three new victims, for travelers usually drowned in the river. But Death was cunning. He pretended to congratulate the three brothers upon their magic, and said that each had earned a prize for having been clever enough to evade him.

So the oldest brother, who was a combative man, asked for a wand more powerful than any in existence: a wand that must always win duels for its owner, a wand worthy of a wizard who had conquered Death! So Death crossed to an elder tree on the banks of the river, fashioned a wand from a branch that hung there, and gave it to the oldest brother.

Then the second brother, who was an

arrogant man, decided that he wanted to humil-
iate Death still further, and asked for the power
to recall others from Death. So Death picked
up a stone from the riverbank and gave it to
the second brother, and told him that the stone
would have the power to bring back the dead.

And then Death asked the third and youngest brother what he would like. The youngest
brother was the humblest and also the wisest
of the brothers, and he did not trust Death. So
he asked for something that would enable him
to go forth from that place without being followed by Death. And Death, most unwillingly,
handed over his own Cloak of Invisibility.

Then Death stood aside and allowed
the three brothers to continue on their way,

and they did so, talking with wonder of the adventure they had had, and admiring Death's gifts.

In due course the brothers separated, each for his own destination.

The first brother traveled on for a week or more, and reaching a distant village, sought out a fellow wizard with whom he had a quarrel. Naturally, with the Elder Wand as his weapon, he could not fail to win the duel that followed. Leaving his enemy dead upon the floor, the oldest brother proceeded to an inn, where he boasted loudly of the powerful wand he had snatched from Death himself, and of how it made him invincible.

That very night, another wizard crept upon the oldest brother as he lay, wine-sodden, upon his bed. The thief took the wand and, for good measure, slit the oldest brother's throat.

And so Death took the first brother for his own.

Meanwhile, the second brother journeyed to his own home, where he lived alone. Here he took out the stone that had the power to recall the dead, and turned it thrice in his hand. To his amazement and his delight, the figure of the girl he had once hoped to marry, before her untimely death, appeared at once before him.

Yet she was sad and cold, separated from him as by a veil. Though she had returned to the mortal world, she did not truly belong there and suffered. Finally the second brother, driven mad with hopeless longing, killed himself so as truly to join her.

And so Death took the second brother for his own.

But though Death searched for the third brother for many years, he was never able to find him. It was only when he had attained a great

age that the youngest brother finally took off
the Cloak of Invisibility and gave it to his son.
And then he greeted Death as an old friend,
and went with him gladly, and, equals, they
departed this life.

# ALBUS DUMBLEDORE

*on "The Tale of the Three Brothers"*

This story made a profound impression on me as a boy. I heard it first from my mother, and it soon became the tale I requested more often than any other at bedtime. This frequently led to arguments with my younger brother, Aberforth, whose favorite story was "Grumble the Grubby Goat."

The moral of "The Tale of the Three Brothers" could not be any clearer: Human efforts to evade or overcome death are always doomed to disappointment. The third brother in the story ("the humblest and also the wisest") is the only one who understands that, having narrowly escaped Death once, the best he can hope for is to postpone their next meeting for as long as possible. This youngest brother knows that taunting Death — by engaging in violence, like the first brother, or by meddling in the shadowy art of necromancy,[1] like the second brother — means pitting oneself against a wily enemy who cannot lose.

The irony is that a curious legend has grown up around this story, which precisely contradicts the message of the original. This legend holds that the gifts Death gives the brothers — an unbeatable wand, a stone that can bring back the dead, and an Invisibility Cloak that endures

---

1 [Necromancy is the Dark Art of raising the dead. It is a branch of magic that has never worked, as this story makes clear. — JKR]

forever — are genuine objects that exist in the real world. The legend goes further: If any person becomes the rightful owner of all three, then he or she will become "master of Death," which has usually been understood to mean that they will be invulnerable, even immortal.

We may smile, a little sadly, at what this tells us about human nature. The kindest interpretation would be: "Hope springs eternal."[2] In spite of the fact that, according to Beedle, two of the three objects are highly dangerous, in spite of the clear message that Death comes for us all in the end, a tiny minority of the Wizarding community persists in believing that Beedle was

---

2 [This quotation demonstrates that Albus Dumbledore was not only exceptionally well-read in Wizarding terms, but also that he was familiar with the writings of Muggle poet Alexander Pope. — JKR]

sending them a coded message, which is the exact reverse of the one set down in ink, and that they alone are clever enough to understand it.

Their theory (or perhaps "desperate hope" might be a more accurate term) is supported by little actual evidence. True invisibility cloaks, though rare, exist in this world of ours; however, the story makes it clear that Death's Cloak is of a uniquely durable nature.[3] Through all the centuries that have intervened between Beedle's day and our own, nobody has ever claimed to have found Death's Cloak. This is explained away

---

3 [Invisibility cloaks are not, generally, infallible. They may rip, or grow opaque with age, or the charms placed upon them may wear off, or be countered by charms of revealment. This is why witches and wizards usually turn, in the first instance, to Disillusionment Charms for self-camouflage or concealment. Albus Dumbledore was known to be able to perform a Disillusionment Charm so powerful as to render himself invisible without the need for a cloak. — JKR]

by true believers thus: Either the third brother's descendants do not know where their cloak came from, or they know, and are determined to show their ancestor's wisdom by not trumpeting the fact.

Naturally enough, the stone has never been found either. As I have already noted in the commentary for "Babbitty Rabbitty and Her Cackling Stump," we remain incapable of raising the dead, and there is every reason to suppose that this will never happen. Vile substitutions have, of course, been attempted by Dark wizards, who have created Inferi,[4] but these are ghastly puppets, not truly reawakened humans. What is more, Beedle's story is quite explicit

---

4 [Inferi are corpses reanimated by Dark Magic. — JKR]

about the fact that the second brother's lost love

has not really returned from the dead. She has

been sent by Death to lure the second brother

into Death's clutches, and is therefore cold,

remote, tantalizingly both present and absent.[5]

This leaves us with the wand, and here the

obstinate believers in Beedle's hidden message

have at least some historical evidence to back up

their wild claims. For it is the case — whether

because they liked to glorify themselves, or to

intimidate possible attackers, or because they

truly believed what they were saying — that

wizards down the ages have claimed to possess

a wand more powerful than the ordinary, even

---

5 Many critics believe that Beedle was inspired by the Philosopher's
Stone, which makes the immortality-inducing Elixir of Life, when
creating this stone that can raise the dead.

an "unbeatable" wand. Some of these wizards have gone so far as to claim that their wand is made of elder, like the wand supposedly made by Death. Such wands have been given many names, among them the "Wand of Destiny" and the "Deathstick."

It is hardly surprising that old superstitions have grown up around our wands, which are, after all, our most important magical tools and weapons. Certain wands (and therefore their owners) are supposed to be incompatible:

> *When his wand's oak and hers is holly,*
> *Then to marry would be folly.*

or to denote flaws in the owner's character:

*Rowan gossips, chestnut drones,*

*ash is stubborn, hazel moans.*

And sure enough, within this category of unproven sayings we find:

*Wand of elder, never prosper.*

Whether because of the fact that Death makes the fictional wand out of elder in Beedle's story, or because power-hungry or violent wizards have persistently claimed that their own wands are made of elder, it is not a wood that is much favored among wandmakers.

The first well-documented mention of a wand made of elder that had particularly strong and dangerous powers was owned by Emeric, commonly called "the Evil," a short-lived but exceptionally aggressive wizard who terrorized the south of England in the early Middle Ages. He died as he had lived, in a ferocious duel with a wizard known as Egbert. What became of Egbert is unknown, although the life expectancy of medieval duelers was generally short. In the days before there was a Ministry of Magic to regulate the use of Dark Magic, dueling was usually fatal.

A full century later, another unpleasant character, this time named Godelot, advanced the study of Dark Magic by writing a collection of dangerous spells with the help of a wand he described in his notebook as "my moste wicked and subtle friend, with bodie of ellhorn,[6] who

6 An old name for "Elder."

knowes ways of magick moste evile." (*Magick Moste Evile* became the title of Godelot's masterwork.)

As can be seen, Godelot considers his wand to be a helpmeet, almost an instructor. Those who are knowledgeable about wandlore[7] will agree that wands do indeed absorb the expertise of those who use them, though this is an unpredictable and imperfect business; one must consider all kinds of additional factors, such as the relationship between the wand and the user, to understand how well it is likely to perform with any particular individual. Nevertheless, a hypothetical wand that had passed through the hands of many Dark wizards would be likely to

---

7 Such as myself.

have, at the very least, a marked affinity for the most dangerous kinds of magic.

Most witches and wizards prefer a wand that has "chosen" them to any kind of second-hand wand, precisely because the latter is likely to have learned habits from its previous owner that might not be compatible with the new user's style of magic. The general practice of burying (or burning) the wand with its owner, once he or she has died, also tends to prevent any individual wand learning from too many masters. Believers in the Elder Wand, however, hold that because of the way in which it has always passed allegiance between owners — the next master overcoming the first, usually by killing him — the Elder Wand has never been

destroyed or buried, but has survived to accu-
mulate wisdom, strength, and power far beyond
the ordinary.

Godelot is known to have perished in his
own cellar, where he was locked by his mad son,
Hereward. We must assume that Hereward took
his father's wand, or the latter would have been
able to escape, but what Hereward did with
the wand after that we cannot be sure. All that
is certain is that a wand called the "Eldrun[8]
Wand" by its owner, Barnabas Deverill, appeared
in the early eighteenth century, and that Deverill
used it to carve himself out a reputation as a
fearsome warlock, until his reign of terror was
ended by the equally notorious Loxias, who took

_____

8 Also an old name for "Elder."

the wand, rechristened it the "Deathstick," and used it to lay waste to anyone who displeased him. It is difficult to trace the subsequent history of Loxias's wand, as many claimed to have finished him off, including his own mother.

What must strike any intelligent witch or wizard on studying the so-called history of the Elder Wand is that every man who claims to have owned it[9] has insisted that it is "unbeatable," when the known facts of its passage through many owners' hands demonstrate that has it not only been beaten hundreds of times, but that it also attracts trouble as Grumble the Grubby Goat attracted flies. Ultimately,

---

9 No witch has ever claimed to own the Elder Wand. Make of that what you will.

the quest for the Elder Wand merely supports an observation I have had occasion to make many times over the course of my long life, that humans have a knack of choosing precisely those things that are worst for them.

But which of us would have shown the wisdom of the third brother, if offered the pick of Death's gifts? Wizards and Muggles alike are imbued with a lust for power; how many would resist the "Wand of Destiny"? Which human being, having lost someone they loved, could withstand the temptation of the Resurrection Stone? Even I, Albus Dumbledore, would find it easiest to refuse the Invisibility Cloak; which only goes to show that, clever as I am, I remain just as big a fool as anyone else.

# ABOUT THE CHILDREN'S HIGH LEVEL GROUP

*Dear Reader,*

*Thank you very much for buying this unique and special book. I wanted to take this opportunity to explain just how your support will help us to make a real difference to the lives of so many vulnerable children.*

*More than one million children live in large residential institutions across Europe. Contrary to popular belief, most of them are not orphans, but are in care because their families are poor, disabled, or from ethnic minorities. Many of these children have disabilities and handicaps, but often remain without any health or educational interventions. In some cases they do not receive life's basics, such as adequate food. Almost always they are without human or emotional contact and stimulation.*

*To change the lives of institutionalized and marginalized children, and try to make sure that no future generation suffers in this way, J. K. Rowling and I set up the Children's High Level Group (CHLG) charity in 2005. We wanted to give these* abandoned children a voice, to allow their stories to be heard.

The CHLG aims to bring an end to the use of large institutions and promote ways that allow children to live with families — their own, foster, or national adoptive parents — or in small group homes.

The campaign helps around a quarter of a million children each year. We fund a dedicated, independent, child help line that provides support and information to hundreds of thousands of children annually. We also run education activities, including the "Community Action" project in which young people from mainstream education work with special-needs children in institutions; and "Edelweiss," which allows young people who are marginalized and institutionalized to express themselves through their creativity and talents. And in Romania, the CHLG has created a national children's council to represent the rights of children, and which allows them to speak out about their own experiences.

But our reach goes only so far. We need funds to scale up and replicate our work, to reach out into more countries and help even more children who are in such desperate need.

CHLG has a unique character amongst nongovernmental organizations in this field, namely *working with governments and state institutions, civil society (not-for-profit and volunteer organizations, faith groups, child advocacy groups, and lobbyists), professionals, and practical providers of services at a grassroots level.*

*CHLG aims to achieve full implementation of the UN Convention on the Rights of the Child across Europe and ultimately around the world. In only two years, we have already assisted governments to develop strategies to prevent the abandonment of babies in hospitals and to improve the care of children with disabilities and handicaps, and have developed a manual of best practice in deinstitutionalization.*

*We are truly grateful for your support in buying this book. These vital funds will allow CHLG to continue our activities, giving hundreds of thousands more children the chance of a decent and healthy life.*

*To find out more about us and how you can get further involved, please visit www.chlg.org.*

*Thank you,*

*Baroness Nicholson of Winterbourne, MEP*
*Co-Chair of CHLG*

This book was edited by Arthur A. Levine and
art directed by David Saylor. The art for the cover was
created using pastels on toned printmaking paper.
The art for the interiors was created using pen and ink
on paper. The book was designed by Elizabeth B. Parisi
and typeset by Brad Walrod. The text was set in Adobe
Garamond Pro. The book was printed and bound at
Quebecor World in Martinsburg, West Virginia. The
Managing Editor was Karyn Browne; the Continuity
Editor was Cheryl Klein; and the Manufacturing
Director was Meryl Wolfe.